Billy
Beaver

Billy Beaver

Dave and Pat Sargent

Illustrated by
Blaine Sapaugh

Ozark Publishing, Inc.
P.O. Box 228
Prairie Grove, AR 72753

F
Sar   Sargent, Dave
     Billy Beaver, by Dave and Pat Sargent. Illus. by Blaine Sapaugh.
     Ozark Publishing, Inc., 1996.
     51P. Illus. (Animal Pride Series)
     Summary: When Billy is told to leave home, he finds himself alone and scared. After he conquers his fears, along comes Susie.
     1.Beavers. I. Sargent, Pat. II. Title. III. Series.

ISBN Casebound 1-56763-084-7
ISBN Paperback 1-56763-004-9

Ozark Publishing, Inc.
P.O. Box 228
Prairie Grove, AR 72753
Ph: 1-800-321-5671

Printed in the United States Of America

Inspired by

our love of animals and the great
outdoors and a desire to share our
feelings with others.

Dedicated to

my friend, James Rowe.

Foreword

Billy is shocked when his mother tells him that he has to leave home and fend for himself. He soon finds himself alone in the woods. Scared but brave, Billy struggles to conquer his fears.

Contents

Billy
Beaver

One

Billy Beaver Leaves Home

I t was a warm summer morning, and Billy Beaver woke
from a deep sleep. He lay on his

bed and stretched and yawned, then rubbed his eyes, trying to wake up. After a few minutes, he was fully awake.

Billy made his way to the lodge entrance and swam through the door. When he reached the surface of the pond, he could feel the warm rays from the morning sun hitting his head.

After swimming for several minutes, Billy Beaver decided it was time to eat. He swam to the shore and slowly made his way to the nearby trees. Because he wasn't sure about what kind of bark he wanted for breakfast, he started tasting every tree. He came to a large sycamore that had tender bark and a sweet taste that he liked. He ate his fill of sycamore bark. Then he went back to the pond to play *"Catch Me if You Can"* with the fish and the frogs.

The water was crystal clear, and it was easy for Billy to spot his friend, Joe Frog. Billy started chasing Joe Frog. Joe could turn fast in the water and hide under a small rock, and he did just that.

Billy Beaver swam back and forth several times trying to find Joe Frog. Joe was lying under a small rock watching Billy Beaver when Sally Catfish came swimming by. Sally Catfish loved to play with Billy Beaver and Joe Frog. She swam over to Billy, and Joe Frog swam from his hiding place so they could play together.

The three of them swam around the pond for a long time before tiring out. They all agreed it was time for a short nap. Then they would meet later in the afternoon.

Billy Beaver swam back to the lodge and lay on his bed. He soon fell asleep. Sometime later he was awakened by a lot of chattering. It took a couple of minutes for him to wake up enough to see that his dad was saying something to his mom.

Billy Beaver heard his dad ask his mom, "Did you tell Billy what I told you to tell him?"

"No," Billy's mom replied, "I'm going to tell him as soon as he wakes up from his nap."

Billy's dad said, "I'm going to take a short nap. I hope the wind dies down so that I can chew down that elm tree near the dam. There are two good limbs on that tree that I need to finish repairs on the dam. Then maybe those pesky raccoons won't be able to tear up the dam anymore." Then, Billy's dad stretched out on his bed and went to sleep.

After a few minutes, Billy got up and started to leave the lodge. He heard his mother call, "Billy, I need to talk to you. Meet me by the willow tree. I'll be there as soon as I finish cleaning the floor."

Billy Beaver waited patiently under the willow tree for his mother. When she got there, she sat down beside him and said, "Billy, it's time for you to leave the lodge and the pond."

"You are grown now, and you must find a stream of your own where you can build a dam and a lodge for yourself. In time, you'll find yourself a girlfriend. Your father has taught you all you need to know about building a dam and a lodge. I am your mother, and I'll always love you, but

the time has come for you to go,
and nothing can change that. So,
go now, and God bless you,
Billy."

Billy watched as his mother
swam back toward the lodge. He

lay there on the bank with his head resting on his front feet. Large tears fell from his eyes. He thought to himself, "Where can I go? All my friends are here."

Realizing that he was no longer welcome and that he couldn't stay, he said, "Bye, Joe Frog. Bye, Sally Catfish. Bye, Mama and Daddy. I love you."

Billy Beaver turned and headed toward the mountains to find a stream of his own.

10

Two

Alone in the Woods

A s Billy Beaver made his way up the mountain, he found the traveling slow and tiring. His feet were sore from walking on rocks. He had never been on land for more than a few minutes at a time.

Billy was very hungry, and, realizing that it would soon be dark, he decided to find a tree with a good-tasting bark for his dinner. He could use a lot of the wood shavings for his bed.

For the first time in his life, he would be sleeping in the open. He would not have the comfort and security of the lodge.

As darkness drew near, Billy became frightened. He heard sounds of wild animals that he had never heard before. The wolves and coyotes were howling, and he heard the owls, "Whooo-whooo."

Billy lay there quiet and still, listening to the new sounds. With every new sound, his heart beat faster. He knew that there was no way he could sleep. He hoped that the sun would soon come up.

Time passed ever so slowly, and from time to time, Billy could

hear the distant cry of a mountain lion. Then he heard leaves and brush rattling. The sound kept coming closer and closer. The moon was now high in the sky, but the trees wouldn't let enough light shine through for him to see what was coming. The sounds grew nearer and nearer.

Billy was now in a panic, for whatever was coming was now only a few yards away, and his only defense was his sharp teeth. The sounds were now directly in front of him. Suddenly, he heard a voice ask, "Billy Beaver, what are you doing here?"

To Billy's surprise, he saw

Jack Moose standing there. He had seen Jack Moose drink from the beaver pond many times. Billy Beaver said, "I was sent away to find a home of my own. I am no longer welcome at the pond or the lodge."

Jack Moose said, "I guess that means you are grown now, Billy Beaver."

Billy asked, "What are you doing here, Jack Moose?"

"I'm looking for a good warm place to lie down where I can spend the rest of the night," Jack Moose replied.

"Why don't you spend the rest of the night here?" Billy Beaver asked. Then he added, "I'll help you keep warm."

Jack Moose chuckled, and knowing how scared Billy was, he said, "I guess this is as good a place as any." Then he lay down beside Billy Beaver. Billy snuggled

up close to Jack Moose, and they both fell asleep.

The next morning at first light, Billy woke up to find that Jack Moose had already left. Billy knew that Jack Moose always got up early. Billy Beaver was hungry, so he started searching for some good tender bark to eat. He finally found some. It wasn't his favorite, but it would have to do for now. After eating his fill, he made his way to the top of the mountain. Once on top, Billy could see everywhere. He could see for miles in every direction.

Billy looked into the valley on the other side of the mountain and saw a small stream of water flowing gently through the valley. He thought it might make a good place for a pond. He ran as fast as he could down the mountainside. Once he reached the stream, he sat and looked for a long time. He was studying the lay of the land and the speed of the water. He knew that these things were very important when building a dam.

Billy Beaver started checking the trees. He had to make sure there would be enough trees near the stream to build a dam for the pond and a lodge to live in.

Once Billy was satisfied that everything he needed was there, he cut down a small tree with his sharp teeth and pulled it to the middle of the stream where he started building a dam.

Three

Billy Finds a Wife

Billy Beaver worked hard on the dam every day. He cut all the trees near the stream first and cut them into pieces just so-so to build the dam.

Every day the dam was a little larger. Before long, Billy had a small pond. It wasn't very big at first, but it was large enough to swim around in. After a few more days, the dam had backed the water up to the place where Billy Beaver wanted to build his lodge. Now, he would have to work on the dam part of the time, and part of the time would be spent on the lodge.

As Billy laid the first limbs to start the lodge, a smile covered his face. He knew it wouldn't be much longer until he would have a nice, warm place to live. He also knew that when wintertime came, he couldn't survive unless he had a lodge.

Billy worked hard and fast because he wanted to get the lodge finished. He was tired of sleeping in the open, and he was always afraid that a wild animal would attack during the night.

Another two weeks passed, and Billy finally had the dam tall enough so that it would make water back up all around his lodge. That night, for the first time in almost four months, Billy slept in the comfort and security of a lodge.

The next morning when Billy
Beaver woke up, he left his lodge
to find some breakfast. When he
got outside, he noticed a chill in
the air. It was much colder than
usual, and everything was covered
with frost. Billy knew that hard
winter wasn't far off, and he still
had a lot of work to do.

After eating breakfast, Billy went to work on the dam. He figured it would take about another month to finish it. It was almost lunchtime before he stopped to rest and eat his lunch. While he was eating, he saw another beaver coming toward the pond. Billy Beaver had worked hard on his pond, and he wasn't going to share it with anyone. As the beaver got closer, Billy showed his teeth and began beating his tail against the ground in anger. Now, only a few feet away, the beaver stopped and lay on the ground. Billy could see that the beaver was crying.

He stopped displaying his anger
and walked up close to the beaver.
He asked, "What's wrong?"

Billy could tell that the
beaver was a girl. She said, "I'm
all alone, and I have no place to
live."

"Well, why don't you build a
pond and a lodge?" Billy asked.

"I don't know how," she
replied.

Billy thought for a minute or so, then asked, "What's your name?"

"My name's Susie Beaver," she replied in a soft voice, then asked, "What's yours?"

"My name is Billy Beaver," he stated proudly.

"You sure have a nice pond, Billy," she said.

"Thank you," Billy answered. "I like it, but there's still a lot of work to do."

Susie said, "If you want, I could help you."

Billy thought for a minute, then said, "I guess that will be all right."

Billy Beaver and Susie Beaver started working on the dam together. Under beaver law, once beavers start working together on a dam for their pond and lodge, they become husband and wife.

Billy and Susie finished the

dam before hard winter set in, and
they lived happily ever after.

Beaver Facts

A beaver is a furry animal with a wide, flat tail that looks like a paddle. Beavers are known for their skill at cutting down trees with their strong front teeth. They eat bark and use the branches to build dams and lodges (homes) in the water. Beavers almost always seem to be busy working. For this reason, we often call a hard-working person an "eager beaver" or say he is as "busy as a beaver."

Beavers live in rivers, streams, and fresh-water lakes near woodlands. They are excellent swimmers and divers. A beaver can swim underwater for one-half mile and can hold its breath for fifteen minutes.

There are more beavers in the United States and Canada than anywhere else in the world. Beavers are also found in Asia and Europe.

Beavers were probably the most hunted animals in North America from the early 1600s through the 1800s. The pioneers and Indians ate beaver meat and traded the furs for things they needed. In the late 1600s, a man could trade twelve beaver skins for a rifle. One beaver skin would buy four pounds of shot, or a kettle, or a pound of tobacco.

The United States and Canadian governments passed

laws to protect the beaver; and today, beavers, like many other wild animals, can be hunted only at certain times of the year.

North American beavers are three to four feet long, including the tail, and weigh from forty to sixty pounds. Unlike most other kinds of mammals, beavers keep growing throughout their lives. Most beavers look larger than they really are because of their humped backs and thick fur. Thousands of years ago, the beavers of North America were about seven and a half feet long, including the tail—almost as long as the grizzly bears. No one knows why these huge beavers disappeared.

The beaver has a broad head with large and powerful jaws. Its rounded ears and small nostrils can close tightly to keep water out. A beaver has three eyelids on each eye. Two outer eyelids, one upper and one lower, fit around the eye. A transparent inner eyelid slides down over the eye and lets the animal see under water. On land, it protects the eye from sharp twigs when the animal cuts trees. The beaver cannot see well, and depends on its keen hearing and smell to warn it of danger.

A beaver has twenty teeth—four strong, curved front teeth for gnawing, and sixteen back teeth for chewing. The front teeth, called incisors, have a bright orange outer covering that is very hard. The back part of the incisors is much softer. When a beaver gnaws, the back part of its incisors wears down much faster than the front part. As a result, these teeth have a sharp, chisel-like edge. The incisors never wear out because they keep growing throughout the animal's life. The back teeth have flat, rough edges and stop growing when the beaver is about two years old.

The beaver's legs are short, and its feet are black. Tough skin, with little hairs, covers the feet. Each front paw ends in five toes  that have long, thick claws. A beaver uses its claws to dig up the roots of bushes and trees for food. When swimming, the animal usually makes tight fists of its front paws and holds them against its chest. Sometimes, when a beaver swims through underwater brush or grass, it uses its front paws to push the plants aside.

The back feet are larger than  the front ones, and may be six to seven inches long. The toes are webbed and end in strong claws. Two claws on each foot are split. The beaver uses these splits to comb its fur. The webbed feet serve as flippers and help make the animal a powerful swimmer and diver.

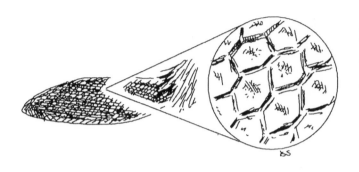

The tail of a beaver is one of the animal's most interesting features. The stiff, flat tail looks like a paddle. It is about twelve inches long, six to seven inches wide, and three-fourths inch thick. A small part of the tail nearest the beaver's body has the same kind of fur as the body. The rest of the tail is covered with black, scaly skin and has only a few stiff hairs. The beaver uses its tail to steer when it swims. The tail is also used as a prop when the animal stands on its hind legs to eat or to cut down trees. A beaver slaps its tail on the water to make a loud noise to warn other beavers of danger.

Beaver fur varies from shiny dark brown to yellowish brown. It looks black when wet. A beaver's coat has an underfur that helps keep the beaver comfortable in the water. This fur traps air and holds it close to the animal's skin. The trapped air acts as a protective blanket that keeps the beaver warm, even in icy water. The beaver's coat has long, heavy guard hairs that lie over the under-fur and protect it.

Beavers usually live in family groups. As many as twelve beavers may make up a family, but generally there are six or fewer. The group includes the adult male and female, the young born the year before, and the new-born.

Beavers live as long as twelve years. Their enemies include bears, lynxes, otters, wolverines, wolves, and man. A beaver avoids these enemies by living in the water and by coming out mostly at night to eat or work.

A female beaver carries her young inside her body for about three months before they are born. She has two to four babies at a time. Most young beavers, called kits or pups, are born in April or May. A newborn kit is about fifteen inches long, including its tail, and weighs one-half to one and one-half pounds. The tail is about three and a half inches long. A kit has soft, fluffy fur at birth, and its eyes are open. The young live with their parents for about two years, and then are driven from the family group. These young adults are forced out to make room for the newborn. Beavers rarely fight with each other except in spring, when the two-year-olds are driven away.

Beavers eat the bark, twigs, leaves, and roots of trees and shrubs. Poplar trees, especially aspens and cottonwoods, and willow trees are among their favorites. One acre of poplars can support a family of six beavers for one to two years. Beavers also eat water plants and especially like the roots and tender sprouts of water lilies.

Beavers store food for winter use. They anchor branches and logs under the water near their lodges. In winter, they swim under the ice and eat the bark.

A beaver uses its strong front teeth to cut down trees and to peel off the bark and the branches.

To cut a tree, the beaver stands on its hind legs and uses its tail as a prop. It places its front paws on the tree trunk and turns its head sideways. Then the beaver bites the trunk to make a cut in it. It makes another cut farther down on the trunk. The distance between the two cuts depends upon the size of the tree. The cuts are farther apart on large trees than on small ones. The beaver takes several bites at the cuts to make them deeper. Then the animal pulls off the piece of wood between the cuts with its teeth. It keeps cutting and tearing out pieces of wood until the tree falls. Beaver usually cut the wood away around a tree trunk, but it may cut through the trunk from only one side.

A beaver cannot control the

direction in which the tree falls. It cuts until the trunk starts to break and then runs to safety. The animal usually dives into the water nearby. It waits there until it is sure that no enemies have been attracted by the noise of the falling tree. Then the beaver goes back to work on the tree.

First the animal gnaws the branches off the tree. Then it carries, drags, pulls, pushes, or rolls the log into the water. The beaver stores some branches deep in the water for use as food during the winter. The other branches may be used to enlarge or repair the dam and the lodge. Beavers often work alone, but sometimes several work together.

A whole beaver family, and sometimes beavers from other families, may join in building a dam. Beaver dams are made of logs, branches, and rocks plastered together with mud. Then they add brush and log poles.

They strengthen the dam by placing the poles so that the tips lean in the same direction as the water flows. The beavers plaster the tops and sides of the poles with more mud, stones, and wet plants. They do most of this work with their front teeth and front paws. They bring mud from the river bottom by holding it against their chests with their front paws.

The beavers build their dam so that the top is above the water. Some dams are more than one thousand feet long. Beavers may keep their dams in good condition for many years. Most beavers that live in lakes do not build dams, but some build dams across the outlets of small lakes.

Sometimes beavers dig canals so they can move logs to their dams or lodges easily and quickly. The canals are twelve to eighteen inches deep, eighteen to twenty-four inches wide, and may be more than seven hundred feet long. A beaver canal may run from a wooded area to a lake or riverbank, or it may cut across a piece of land that sticks out into the water.

A beaver lodge looks some-what like a tepee. A family of beavers builds its lodge with the same materials and in much the same way as it builds a dam. The lodge may stand on the riverbank or in the water like an island. The tops of most lodges are three to

six feet above the water. Each lodge has several underwater entrances and tunnels, all of which lead to an inside chamber. The floor of the chamber is four to six inches above the water. Here, young beavers can stay warm and dry in winter, and the adults can dry off after bringing in food. Holes between the branches in the ceiling let in fresh air.

The size of the lodge depends on the size of the family and the length of time the beavers have lived there. The animals enlarge and repair the lodge as long as they live in it. Most beavers abandon their lodge only if they have eaten all the food in the area or if too many enemies move nearby.

Beavers that live in large lakes or swift rivers may dig dens in the banks. These dens, like lodges, have underwater entrances and tunnels.